THE LEGACY

OF THE

TWIN FLAME MEADOW

I0553462

by

Spirit Lady Robin Alexis

Introduction, Epigraph, and
Personal Reflection

by

Mary Stephenson

First Printing, 2025
ISBN #979-8-9881534-9-8
Divine Publications

Dedicated

To those who dare to walk the path of Sacred
Union, who come to realize that the true journey
is not about finding "The One," but about finding
and cherishing the Divine within themselves.

To those who choose Agape Love, who
surrender to the fires of transformation, and rise
through devotion to their own becoming.

May this book be a torch in your hand,
a reminder that Love is not something we seek.
It is something we remember.

The Twin Flame path is not a search for another.
It is a return to the wholeness you have always
carried within.

And from that wholeness,
all true Unions are born.

Acknowledgments

With gratitude, I acknowledge

The Spirits of Mount Shasta, for guiding this manuscript into my hands and supporting the creation of this book

The souls known here as Madeline, Adam, and Phoebe, for sharing your Sacred journey during your time in Mount Shasta

Mary Magdalene, for holding integrity in your soul mission

Jesus/Yahshua, for continuing to guide those who choose Agape Love

Mary Stephenson, for your courage in sharing your Twin Flame Journey and narration of the audiobook

Jan Edward, for your editing of the book

Keyth Neso, for recognizing the sacred codes within this story, for contributing the Foreword and narration and audio engineering of the audiobook.

Elizabeth Diane, for the beautiful cover art

All My Love, Robin Alexis

Foreword

by Keyth Neso

Some stories are written with ink. Others are written in memory, waiting for the right moment to be remembered. *The Legacy of the Twin Flame Meadow* is the latter.

This is not just a love story—it is a record of soul evolution.

What you hold in your hands is not fiction. It is testimony. It's the sacred echo of two souls, Madeline and Adam, who walked the crucible of separation, awakening, forgiveness, and return. Their union is not a destination, but an initiatory path—*one many of us are walking now.*

As someone initiated into the teachings of the Nasarean Essenes, I recognize the codes that live in these pages. The sacred union path is not a concept. It is a lineage. Yahshua and Mary Magdalene were co-messiahs, not metaphorically, but literally. He was not her savior. She was not his shadow. They were equals. She prepared the womb. He cleansed the death realms. This is the Divine order being restored.

Madeline and Adam reflect that same arc, through human heartbreak, spiritual surrender, and soul-level vow. Their Meadow is real. Mount Shasta is not metaphor—*it is a planetary temple, a grid point that holds memory of Lemuria, the Magdalene, and the sacred return of Divine Union.*

This book was not "written." It was received. It was remembered. It was translated. And in doing so, it activated a living scripture encoded for this time.

My work—*what I call the Golden Braid*—is to weave the sacred texts of the *Holy Megillah*, Dolores Cannon's transmissions, and the Tarot of the Blue Rose into one continuum. Each golden strand stands as a pillar of truth on its own, however when woven together, they create a harmonious frequency, a sacred chord composed of holy tones that is powerful enough to initiate a collective awakening.

This book is part of that braid.

I invite you to enter this text not as a reader, but as a witness. Let it meet you where you are, but don't be surprised if it begins to shift your internal timeline. It may bring up grief. It may stir memories. It may ask you to lay something down. Let it. The Meadow can only be entered with an open heart.

You are not here to wait for love. You are here to become it.

Only love and ever onward,

Keyth Neso

The Twin Flame Meadow is an etheric realm, a soul space beyond time, where two Divine counterparts return to one another across lifetimes. It is here, in this Sacred field, that Twin Flames choose each other again and again, through heartbreak and healing, through lifetimes of separation and reunion.

Each return is an initiation. Through the fires of forgiveness, the alchemy of redemption, and the unwavering call of Divine Love, the Twin Flames are forged into Sacred Union. When their souls are fully ripened by Love's journey, they are permitted to meet in the Heaven-on-Earth meadow of Mount Shasta, California.

There, in the presence of angels and guides, their eternal vow is renewed. They are united in holy matrimony, anchored in the Sacred harmony of Divine masculine and Divine feminine. And their Union is written not just in memory, but in the Book of Love itself.

If you are reading this, you are already on the path.

The question is, *Will you walk it?*

Contents

Preface

When my husband Bob and I first came to Mount Shasta, it was meant to be a two-week vacation. He ended up wanting to stay for a month. At the time, however, we couldn't find a place that would host our pets. So, he persuaded me to rent a house– *for a year.*

We didn't want to buy new furniture for our one-year adventure, so we began to explore yard sales, estate sales, and garage sales. At one estate sale, we bought some really cool old furniture, not realizing until we got home that the drawer in the beautiful French desk didn't open. Though we tugged and pulled and shook it, nothing would get the drawer unstuck. Our son, who can fix anything, couldn't get it open. We hired a locksmith who couldn't get it open without damaging it. So, we resigned ourselves to the fact that we had purchased a beautiful French desk with a drawer that couldn't open.

Ten years later (yes, we never left Mount Shasta), I decided to move the desk. Lo and behold, as I was shifting it back and forth, it wobbled in such a way that the drawer flew open, and I saw what had been stuck. Inside the drawer were old papers with typewritten and handwritten letters and poems. They had been wedged in so tightly that they had jammed the drawer shut for all those years. Who knew how long they had been there.

Before the internet and cell phones, life was vastly different—*people had "pen pals" with whom they corresponded regularly.* The couple who wrote these pages lived in a time when people at a distance from one another communicated through letters, correspondence handwritten with paper and pen. These personal messages were enclosed in envelopes and sealed for privacy. After addressing the envelopes to the intended recipients and affixing them with a postage stamp, they were sent through the mail and delivered by hand. In times of war, letters could take months to reach their destination.

I carefully removed the papers and, after looking closer, realized that these were not just letters. Some were typed pages of a manuscript, complete with chapter numbers, along with a note with explicit instructions not to publish until after her death.

I thought I was uncovering someone's past, a long-lost Love story, giving me a private window into a couple's soul-level bond. I had no idea the depth of what I was holding. Yet I knew the letters held something Sacred. I felt the weight of that the moment I saw them, transmissions forgotten by time, yet pulsing like the beat of a heart.

As a psychic medium and clairvoyant, I receive images and messages from souls who have passed. I have an immediate knowing, and I know what I know. In the moment I held the pages, my heart burst open with the recognition of a soul purpose. I suddenly was filled with insight and a vision of a very happy couple. It was clear that they had decided that it was time for their story to come alive again and be told. And they had chosen me to tell it.

But, it wasn't the first time this message had come through—*only the first time I was ready to receive it.*

When Bob and I had talked about moving to Mount Shasta, I hadn't wanted to go. But my soul knew. It was calling me here. And this was why.

Slowly, across the span of time and awakenings, what unfolded was far more than I could have ever imagined.

And I began to remember.

The couple's daughter, Phoebe, had died before putting together her parents' book. When she began to communicate with me, I understood.

Those pages weren't someone else's letters and book. They were mine.

Phoebe and I are not separate people. We are parallel expressions of the same soul.

She was channeling the energy through me to guide me to finish putting together what she had started and not finished.

She was the child who saw beyond the veil.
I am the woman who dared to open the drawer.

Phoebe lived the story.
I arrived later to tell it, by putting together the pages of her mother's book.

Some stories don't begin when they're written.

They begin when they're remembered.

It is my deep honor to share this gift with you,

in gratitude for being part of their remembrance,

and perhaps, your own.

Introduction to The Twin Flame Meadow

by Mary Stephenson

There are stories hidden beneath the surface of our lives—stories that were never lost, only waiting for the hearts that would remember them and the souls that would stir at their calling.

This is one of those stories.

This book is not only a record of the past. It is an eternal blueprint hidden in plain sight, a map of Love's initiatory path.

These two souls of humble origins raised in the quiet simplicity of 1930s America were not rulers or mystics, but ordinary people with an extraordinary contract. They carried the weight of past lives in a world that did not yet understand their connection. Madeline and Adam have walked this Earth again and again, taking new names, living new lives, moving through the Sacred cycles of departure and return.

Their love is not mere romance, but a mirror of truth that the Sacred Union of soul counterparts weaves through all of time. Their journey, forged in the quiet struggles and tender triumphs of everyday life was not easy. Raw, real, and tested by fire, it carries the archetypal currents of Divine Love's promise—*the call to reunite, heal, and rise beyond separation.*

Madeline and Adam's story is here to remind us that Twin Flames are not beings of myth or legend. They are people who live among us— growing, stumbling, and choosing each other again and again, even when the world does not yet recognize the sacredness of their bond.

In their human imperfections, in their perseverance through love and loss, they show us the map– *not in ancient scripts, but etched into the beating heart of life itself* – a map that leads beyond romance, beyond suffering, and into the luminous field of Divine Union.

They whisper to us that Love is not just romance, not merely physical, but the greatest spiritual initiation of all.

And now, their story and Love letters are revealed– whispers across dimensions, encoded with light, tenderness, and truth.

As you walk through these pages, you are invited to not only witness the journey of Madeline and Adam, but yours, as well.

For Love is the true alchemy. And every soul willing to choose Love again and again becomes part of the living legacy of the Twin Flame Meadow.

Who's Who

A Guide for the People and Souls Who Shaped this Legacy

Madeline – Protagonist and Twin Flame of Adam. A woman on a journey of empowerment and remembrance, Madeline represents the Divine feminine principle of fierce Love and Sacred memory, and the reclaiming of her soul's voice across timelines. Her journey is both personal and universal, calling women everywhere to remember who they truly are.

Adam – Protagonist and Twin Flame of Madeline. Adam embodies the Divine masculine in evolution, moving through pain, separation, and loss. Healing and awakening through Love into wholeness. His transformation is central to the healing of the collective masculine energy.

Phoebe – The daughter of Adam and Madeline. A gifted medium with spiritual sight and messages from beyond, she is the bridge between worlds. Phoebe channels guidance from the unseen, carrying forth the legacy of both her parents.

Sarah – Madeline's grandmother. A quiet anchor of ancestral wisdom and grounding presence of feminine lineage, Sarah holds the ancestral thread that connects the past to the future.

Frank – Madeline's grandfather and Sarah's husband. A steady, nurturing presence whose Love shaped generations.

Thelma – Madeline's mother. Her struggles with societal expectations became the catalyst for Madeline's soul awakening and reclamation of sovereignty.

Alfred – Madeline's father. Like Adam, Alfred represents earthly roots and karmic legacy. He carries the imprint of a wounded masculine lineage, revealing how both fathers and Lovers are asked to remember, repair, and rise.

Mary Magdalene – Ascended master and Sacred teacher of Divine feminine wisdom. Mary is the embodiment of Sacred feminine leadership. As guide, mirror, and mentor to Madeline, she offers timeless wisdom and compassion in the journey of soul remembrance.

Jesus (Yahshua) – Ascended master, Divine Twin of Magdalene, Sacred masculine teacher.

Yahshua's presence as a spiritual guide of unconditional Love and awakening is not one of dogma, but of deep knowing and Divine Love, reminding both Madeline and Adam of their own Divine nature.

Robin Alexis – Psychic clairvoyant, channel, medium, and spiritual scribe. Through Phoebe, Robin receives and shares the souls' transmissions of Adam and Madeline. She discovered the manuscript and birthed this story into the world through her soul agreement with Madeline and Adam. In the story, Phoebe and Robin are revealed to be soul expressions of the same being– *two lives, one soul path.*

Mary Stephenson – Healer, guide, and witness to this Sacred unfolding. Through the birthing of this book, via the channel of Robin Alexis, Madeline and Adam requested that Mary carry the torch of their lineage, serving as a way-shower and guide for those called to walk the Twin Flame path in this era. Mary accepts this responsibility with humility, reverence, and a heart wide open to Love's higher calling.

Note to the Reader

The beginning of this Love story is told by Madeline, channeled through her daughter, Phoebe.

Madeline is a woman who never felt safe in life. Imagine having lived under such strict societal expectations of what "good" meant that she preferred death over revealing her truths.

Unfortunately, the place that our caretakers were stuck in their development becomes an internal paradigm where we, their children, too become stuck.

"The greatest burden a child must bear is the unlived life of the parents."

Carl Jung

Madeline Speaks

I was born into a lineage of women who knew how to survive. But they didn't always know how to Love themselves– or their daughters. My name is Madeline, and I'm telling you my story now from the other side, through Phoebe's hands. Death didn't end my voice. If anything, it set it free.

My grandmother Sarah was a woman of quiet strength. She grew up in Mount Shasta, where Saturday night dinners almost always included baked beans. On one such night, her parents invited a guest they had chosen as a potential suitor. As the oldest daughter, Sarah was expected to help serve the dinner.

Nervous and eager to impress, she tripped, spilling the entire dish of beans across the floor. Humiliated under her parents' scolding gaze, she burst into tears.

After dinner, the guest, Frank, gently pulled her aside and said, "If you marry me, you can spill the beans– or anything else– whenever you want."

That was his proposal, and she accepted. They married in 1898.

Sarah was the kind of woman one adored without persuasion. She baked, she prayed, and she held her family together with dignity. I once wrote her a Christmas poem– childish, but sincere– and I meant every word of it. In my heart, she's still on a pedestal.

But my mother? That's another story.

After graduating high school, my mother took a job at the local telephone company, housed on the third floor of a building in downtown Mount Shasta. On the second floor below her was the Power Company, where the town's linemen gathered each morning with cigarettes in hand, their laughter echoing through the halls.

Among them was Alfred, my father.

These linemen were considered the town's most eligible bachelors. Local girls flirted with them by snitching their silk scarves from them. Wearing one meant that you were "spoken for" and gave the man an excuse to retrieve it from you. My mother said that when she stole Alfred's scarf and he came to claim it, it smelled so good that she wanted to keep it. He promised to buy her a bottle of the scent, Chanel No. 5. She laughed. That Christmas, he did just that.

Along with the bottle of Chanel was another gift, a bag of sand. Putting her hand inside, she felt a box. When she opened the box, she saw a diamond ring. And that was the beginning of a 63-year marriage.

I'm grateful that they were happy. However, my relationship with my mother was far more complicated. Even here beyond the veil, I feel the resentment. That energy never quite dissolved.

I remember shopping for school clothes as a young girl. I wasn't allowed to speak, only try on what was picked for me. No one asked what I liked. No one asked if I was comfortable. I didn't like being told what to do or what to wear, but obedience dominated self-expression.

My mother was so unaware of who I was as a soul. Somewhere deep in my childhood chest, I made a vow. No one would ever control me again– not even God Himself.

That is where I got the courage to write to Adam.

We had dated in high school. He was kind and steady. When my family moved out of state, and Adam went off to Korea, we lost touch.

Years later, from a desire to reclaim something– maybe him, maybe myself– I wrote to him.

The letter that follows is naïve, maybe, but sincere.

And it changed everything.

June 1950

Dear Adam,

Find a comfortable chair, an extra few minutes, and a cold glass of water. This letter may surprise you as much as it does me. Ever since returning from Oregon, I've wanted to write to you, but never dared.

Now, after seven months, I've finally mustered the courage. I hope you don't mind.

I thought you might be lonely over there. But after seeing some of those movies, I'm not so sure. Still, if you'd like to write, please do. I'll answer.

Graduation week is here! Can you believe it? I'm so proud. We took our class trip to Gold Beach, Oregon, and had a wonderful time. The senior ball was Friday. It was magical. And tomorrow is the big day. A few of us kids are going out to celebrate. I want to dance, but I don't know what the others will want to do.

How's life where you are? I saw your name in the paper two weeks ago. You must be doing well to have graduated from Intelligence Corps School. It sounded fascinating. If you reply, please tell me more about it.

You probably know that my brother Dick is married now, to a woman he met in the service! They're very happy. You better watch out, or you might meet your future wife there, too. I hope, for Heaven's sake, that you're not already married! Please let me know if you are.

Writing to you is harder than I expected. I thought it would be easy, but I don't know what to say. I remember how our letters used to sound. If you do decide to write, please send a picture. Have you changed?

A few of us went swimming today. The water was freezing, so I didn't go all the way in. Guess that makes me a sissy.

How much longer do you have in the service? Oh, and congratulations! I was expecting to write to Private Adam, but now you're Corporal Adam. You're making your way in the world. Are you planning to make the service your career?

I do hope you'll write back.

Please, Adam, if you would like a pen pal, write to me. I'll be waiting. If you'd rather not, please let me know.

Always,
Madeline (in case you forgot)

He was somewhere on the front lines of Korea, and I was a girl in Mount Shasta trying to sound breezy and brave. I thought I was flirting. Really, I was hoping he'd remember me, hoping he hadn't already found someone else. I didn't know the horrors he was living through.

That letter– so light in tone, so naïve– landed in the middle of a war zone.

And somehow, he wrote back.

We exchanged letters for months. Eventually, we became engaged.

But while he was on another tour, I made a terrible mistake.

At hairdressing school, I met a man. He was older and charming, and I thought it was Love. I returned Adam's ring. I soon discovered that man only wanted my youth. When the illusion shattered, I begged my brother to come get me. He did. I wrote to Adam again, apologizing, begging for forgiveness.

He forgave me.

When his ship docked after the war, I was there waiting—eight and a half months pregnant with another man's child. Adam didn't flinch. He married me and adopted my son when he was born. We named him after Adam's best friend in the war.

Seven months later, our daughter was born. Premature. I told everyone that life demanded such performances.

Our marriage was not built on ease or fantasy. We were tired, stretched thin, trying to survive in a world that didn't care about our wounds.

We had a third child. If abortions had been legal, we would have terminated the pregnancy. But she came. And she was strange. Phoebe saw dead people. She spoke of past lives. She talked about aliens. We were Christians, wondering where she had picked up all that nonsense.

But now, Phoebe is the reason I can tell this story.

Our life wasn't all struggle. We had sweet moments. But the darkness– *Adam's trauma, the war, his silence*– it all eventually caught up with us. And when it did, it came like a tidal wave, crashing on top of Adam.

He lost himself– fully and profoundly.

You'll read about that in the pages that follow. But let me say this now. We made it. We chose to keep choosing each other. We built joy where there had been despair. We taught ourselves how to dance– in the hallway, in the kitchen, and in the quiet.

Our story is not perfect. But it's whole.

And maybe, that's the greater miracle. We found a way to build joy. Yet, the shadows of the past were not entirely gone. A storm was brewing on the horizon, a storm that would test us in ways we never imagined.

When Adam finally broke, it wasn't all at once, but slowly, like a mountain splitting down the middle from years of pressure.

One night in September of 1993, he started hearing voices—*clear and constant voices that told him things*—things he believed.

Then, Adam stopped being Adam.

He stopped sleeping and stayed up all night writing. He wrote pages and pages of backward scripture, gibberish, and rage. He wandered the woods. He thought our dog was possessed. He claimed to be Jesus of Nazareth.

I begged him to see a doctor. I pleaded. But he insisted that the voices were from God, that his words had meaning, that I didn't understand.

And he was right. I didn't.

There were nights when he pulled me out of bed to read his pages. On one of those nights, he shook me awake, his eyes glassy and wild. On another night, he raised our little dog, Rosie, high above his head, shaking and raving. Later, he smashed her into a tree, attempting to kill her. Rosie was maimed so badly that, even though I took her to the vet, she died.

Adam wasn't the man I'd known for forty-two years. He was a stranger wearing my husband's face.

Eventually, it all came to a head. The voices had taken full control, and he crashed the car over and over again into our neighbor's house.

The police came and took him to the hospital. Phoebe rode with him. He trusted her. I wasn't allowed in at first. He didn't want me– *only Phoebe*.

Adam's grandfather had died of a brain tumor, and the doctors considered that Adam had genetic brain cancer. His half-sister, Nyssa, joined the team. She was a clinical psychologist. Everyone had answers– *everyone except me.* The hospital staff kept me at a distance. I visited, but he barely knew me.

I felt invisible. Erased.

The team ruled out the tumor and diagnosed Adam with a nervous breakdown. They admitted him to a psychiatric ward and said that time would tell if he would recover.

I was furious, and heartbroken, and so, so tired. Phoebe was the one who stayed. Adam only looked for Phoebe. She saw him. She soothed him. Her presence brought something I could not. Perhaps I had too much history with him, too much pain.

Eventually, with medication and therapy, he began the long road back. When he finally came home, he was heavily subdued with pills.

But, I wasn't ready to give up. I knew he would return to himself—*eventually, partially, enough.*

I drove him to a piece of land near the family farm that he had lost in a cruel inheritance twist. I showed him the oak tree that his parents had planted the day he was born, and I read a bible verse. It was about his resurrection is what the acorn is to the oak tree.

> *"God's kingdom is like an acorn that a farmer plants. It is quite small as seeds go, but in the course of years, it grows into a huge oak tree, and eagles build nests in it."*

"Let's build something new here," I told him, "You'll never have the old land. But you can have this."

He cried.

That was the surrender.

And I knew he was still in there.

I taught him to dance. He resisted at first, saying it was sinful. I said, *"Stop being miserable, Adam."*

And he did.

We danced down the hallway, instead of arguing in it. We built a garden, a life, a rhythm. We chose to stop making misery our religion. We gave cucumbers to the single mom at McDonald's and donuts to the police.

He gave me joy again. And I gave him peace.

At our 60th anniversary, our granddaughter asked us how we lasted.

I said, "Perseverance."

Adam said, *"Jesus."*

Both were true. And both were enough.

Our story isn't clean. But it's honest. And now that I'm gone, I can tell you the rest.

I Loved him– *even when I didn't understand him– even when he didn't understand me.*

And we both learned that Love– *when chosen again and again*– is the holiest miracle of all.

Message to the Reader:

While Adam and I were devoted Christians, and Yahshua (Jesus) remains our Beloved teacher, Twin Flame Love is not confined to any one religion. No matter how you name the Divine– *be it God, Source, Beloved, or something else*– this Sacred frequency of eternal Love is available to all. The soul does not ask for labels. It only longs to return to truth.

Phoebe Explains And Adam Writes a Letter

G rowing up as their daughter, I saw how
their Union was molded by a culture in
which religious doctrine often dictated that a
husband's word was law. My mother's strength
fiercely resisted that outdated notion, and she
was the grounding force, especially in those
early years of conflict. But, beneath the surface
were the shadows of abuse, infidelity, and the
heavy weight of things unspoken.

My father's breakdown had marked a turning
point. It ruptured the illusion of control and
exposed the survival patterns he had inherited
around Love, leadership, and masculinity. That
unraveling, painful as it was, became the
doorway to something new.

In time, he turned away from a version of
religion rooted in guilt and suffering, toward a
spirituality centered on joy, redemption, and
inner resurrection. He began to see that true
partnership– *Divine Union*– is not about

hierarchy, but equality, not about control, but co-creation.

Looking back, I can see that I served as a generational pattern-breaker, holding space as my parents stumbled, softened, and eventually found a path back to each other. Their Love, reborn through struggle, began to reflect something Sacred.

Theirs was the Divine marriage of the inner masculine and feminine—*what my father came to recognize as Christ Consciousness.*

After my mother's passing, he couldn't wait to unlock the drawer and read the manuscript that she had hidden. When he did, he was filled with deep longing to respond to her, but he didn't know if that was possible, or how to do it.

As the days and weeks passed, he began to feel her presence in new ways. He wanted to know what she looked like now. I told him that she looked the same as she did when they first dated in high school. We found an old photo of her, and he looked at it, hoping it would help him feel her.

With my quiet encouragement, he started to reflect on the journey they had shared. And I began to show him how to know what her energy felt like and how to discern the difference between her energy and his. I taught him to listen to himself and then to ask her, *"Is this your energy, or someone else's, or a combination?"*

I told him that it was important not to take in someone else's energy and told him, *"If it's someone else's, you need to give it back."* I showed him how to manage the energies, how to ground himself, and how to realize when he was feeling her.

My father got very good at knowing when she was present. He strengthened his clairsentient and clairaudient abilities and was working on clairvoyance.

With a little nudging from me, he found the courage to say what had never been said. Pulling out their cassette tape recorder, he began to speak to her through the microphone—*actually, he yelled into the microphone.*

As his final offering to her, this letter—*his words* — is part reflection, part apology, part vow. These are the words of a man who came to understand what Love truly asks of us and– *ultimately*– what it gives us in return.

Madeline,

You're gone now. Dead and gone, as they say. But it's not what I expected.

Of course, I miss you– terribly. But with Phoebe helping us stay connected, I've learned to feel you in my arms, hear your voice in my heart. And maybe– just maybe– I'm becoming clairvoyant like she is. We'll see.

I just wanted to thank you, for sticking by me during my breakdown, for choosing to stay when everything fell apart. We both did things we weren't proud of, but, thank God, we stopped rehashing the past. We chose forgiveness. We chose Love. We chose each other.

That choice saved us, didn't it?

We were fundamental Christians. I thought I was better than everyone else– especially you. I'm so sorry for how cruel I was. I was too busy obeying the written word, parroting the church, thinking righteousness meant control.

And you– well, you were made for presence, not rules.

No wonder you found comfort in the arms of others. They saw you. I didn't. And, a woman like you? You won't put up with being unseen.

But now, I see you.

And more than that– through your eyes, I see me.

Madeline, I realize now that your Love was never about saving me. It was about seeing me. You held a vision of who I truly was, even when I was buried under shame and fear. You stood in your own light so powerfully that eventually, I had no choice but to see mine.

Even in death, you kept teaching me— not with words, but with presence. You whispered my name across the veil, not to pull me back to the past, but to call me forward into the man I was always meant to be.

You never tried to change me. You simply reminded me that I was never broken.

Every time I feel your energy now, soft and fierce and holy, I stand a little taller– not to prove anything– but because I finally understand the man you always believed I could be.

I think about those eagles we used to watch, cartwheeling through the sky. Remember? Locked talons, they were falling through the air, letting go just before they hit the ground, then flying back up again over and over.

That was us, Madeline. That was our human marriage.

Now I see it. What we lived through was a kind of holy preparation. Agape Love isn't just some pretty phrase. It's what you grow into when nothing is left but truth.

I plan to see you again, Madeline, in Heaven. And when I do, I want to marry you again— for real this time. Maybe Jesus will officiate.

See you soon, dear.

With Love,
Adam

But of course, the story does not end there.

As Adam's heart opened across the veil, Madeline was already preparing to answer his call.

Madeline Reveals

C hristians don't typically believe in reincarnation. Nor do they believe in speaking with the dead. Well, surprise! I'm dead. And I can assure you now, from the other side, that those beliefs are, shall we say, a bit limiting.

Fortunately, I have a daughter who is a medium. She talks to the dead as a profession. And now that I'm on this side of the veil, I fully intend to take advantage of that. In life, I dismissed her abilities. For decades, I was skeptical. I even ridiculed her in the times she needed me most. Well, that's her story to tell. But now, from this wider view, I see it all so clearly.

Like many parents, I had no idea what I was doing. Especially in my generation, we weren't taught conscious parenting. Babies often arrived like a surprise burst of fairy dust– *sometimes inconvenient, sometimes unwanted, and often completely unplanned.* That's how Phoebe came to us.

When she was in her forties, her father and I admitted to her that, had abortion been legal at the time, we probably would've made that choice– *not because we didn't want her* —because we felt so unequipped. Our lives were already overextended. A third child pushed everything past the breaking point.

We Loved her, but we resented what she represented– *more responsibility, more expense, more stress.* And to further complicate things, Phoebe was... different, peculiar. She talked about past lives, dead people, aliens. As Christians, we didn't know what to make of it. To put it bluntly—*we thought she was crazy.*

But we were wrong.

Phoebe was– *and is*– a gift from God. She came into this world with abilities we didn't understand and a mission we couldn't see. Thankfully, we began to wake up and know who she truly was before it was too late.

After I passed, I found myself in the arms of Spirit. And wouldn't you know, the first thing I wanted to do was write to Adam, my Beloved. But I didn't initiate. He did.

You see, after I died, Adam found an old manuscript I'd written and hidden in a locked drawer. He must have been waiting for me to kick the bucket, so he could finally read my secrets.

I had poured my truth onto those pages, things I hadn't dared say aloud. I was so nervous about being found a sinner that I never dared to publish it. I wasn't sure if I would be allowed in Heaven if I did.

My purpose in writing the manuscript was for people to understand mental illness. When Adam lost his mind, I endured it, because I didn't know it was mental illness. I didn't know that we should have gone to get help.

And after we finally did, our marriage began to turn around. And it became this beautiful thing, this amazing, transformative Love.

Adam's mental breakdown was the doorway for our spirituality and our understanding that our feelings were the key that unlocked the door. Walking through that door opened us up to all the Love that we never imagined existed. It gave us choices that we never realized we had.

When Adam read the manuscript, his heart cracked wide open. He reached out to me through the microphone of the tape recorder, his voice trembled with grief and Love and hope.

And somehow, I heard him.

Well, I couldn't help but hear him. You may be wondering why he thought yelling into a cassette recorder would work. Maybe it was intuition. Maybe it was Love. Quite probably, it was a habit in the final years of our marriage, born out of yelling so that I could hear him as I grew deaf and refused to wear a hearing aid.

But mostly, he yelled out of earnest.

I responded and told him that I'm not deaf anymore.

Regardless, that letter became a bridge.

Once that door opened, I began transmitting my responses to Phoebe. She'd wake up in the middle of the night, type my words on her typewriter, and show them to Adam. That's how our Love letters began.

Eventually, Phoebe taught Adam how to communicate with me without her– *how to feel me, hear me, know me.* And that's how we reunited across dimensions.

As I've come to realize, our Love wasn't ordinary. It was archetypal. Twin Flames never lose their connection, not even in death. And as strange as this may sound, I've come to understand our story as part of a much larger lineage, one that echoes the Sacred Union of **Mary Magdalene and Jesus/Yahshua**.

Before, I saw Magdalene through the lens of judgment and distortion. I thought she was the repentant sinner, the footnote in a man's gospel. But now, I see her for who she really was.

Mary Magdalene was a high priestess, a Divine feminine teacher, the Beloved of Christ—*walking beside him, not beneath him.*

Their Love was not one of hierarchy. It was a Sacred alchemy– *equal parts power, tenderness, service, and sovereignty.* They were **Twin Flames** in the truest sense– two aspects of Divine consciousness, awakening through Love, devotion, and purpose.

Magdalene didn't just *know* Jesus/Yahshua. She *held* him. She *anointed* him. She *witnessed* his death. And she rose in her own right, to continue the work of Divine Union long after his body was gone. **She was, and remains, a template for what the Awakened Feminine can be.**

Looking back on my life now, I see how my soul was walking a similar path– flawed and fiery– but in service to something greater than I could have ever articulated at the time.

So, yes, I am Madeline. But I am also the echo of Magdalene. And Adam? He may not have walked on water, *but he rose from his own inner tomb.*

Ours is not a story of perfection. It's a story of resurrection.

Before you read the letters I transmitted from beyond the veil to my daughter Phoebe – *who served as my bridge to Adam*– she wants to share a piece of her story with you.

A Note from Phoebe

When my mother began speaking to me after she passed, I wasn't sure I could trust what I was hearing. Grief can play strange tricks on the mind. But the words that came through were undeniably her– funny, sharp, raw, and full of unexpected wisdom.

At first, I was just the messenger. But over time, I realized that through the process, I was also being healed.

Writing these letters from her gave me a chance to know my mother in a way I never could when she was alive. That woman was bound by fear and obligation, but the soul she had evolved into and spoke to me as, was free.

These letters are from *that* Madeline– the free and evolved soul of my mother. It is my honor to share them with you.

Love Letters from Heaven

A **Message from Robin Alexis**

What follows are nine transmissions Madeline sent to Phoebe after passing. Channeled from beyond the veil, each letter reveals a soul awakening to her true nature, her mistakes, her humor, and her eternal Love.

Though directed to Adam—*these letters are meant for all of us*– anyone navigating the tender ache of separation, the mysteries of reunion, and the unexpected liberation that comes when we surrender to Love's deeper current.

Madeline does not preach. She speaks with candor and grace, and often with a wink. Her voice reflects that of another powerful feminine figure, **Mary Magdalene,** who once walked beside Jesus/Yahshua as his Beloved and equal.

Like Mary Magdalene, Madeline's journey is a return to sovereignty, to Love beyond shame, and to the Sacred work of spiritual Union. She invites us to remember—*our healing doesn't end when we die.*

Healing continues through the dimensions, until we remember who we truly are.

These letters are not just messages between Lovers. They are transmissions of remembrance, for all those called to embody the Divine feminine and masculine in Sacred harmony.

Letter One: Seeing the Face of God

Dear Adam,

This is my first Love letter from Heaven to you, my Love.

I had been waiting for you to ask me the question you always carried—
Did I see the face of God?

We were both wondering if I'd gone straight to Hell for being an adulteress. But let me tell you, Heaven is far more forgiving than anyone can imagine.

So, did I see Him?
Not quite in the way you'd expect.

When I died, I was brought to God, but not to a face. There may have been one, but what I saw and felt was a white-gold light– brilliant, fierce, and pure– a radiant strength that lifted me completely out of my physical body. I just left it behind.

And then I entered another body, a lighter one. In this one, I could communicate again– still as me, but refined, clarified, pure.

It was from that place that I finally understood what you were always trying to teach me in life–
Agape Love.

It isn't like this for everyone, you know. But we– we are Twin Flames.
We came into these lives knowing that we would have to walk through fire, alone, and together.

Our path was an initiation– to see if we truly had what it takes to live in eternal Love, and to become living examples of Christ Consciousness.

I see it now.

Yours in Eternity,
Madeline

Letter Two: Mischief School

Dear Adam,

I now know that the letters I sent to you during the war reached you at impossible moments. One of the things you learn here in Mischief School (yes, that's what they call it) is how our actions ripple through others' lives in ways we couldn't imagine.

I was shown the moment you received my Dear John letter. It arrived while you were on a mission, and your unit had run out of ammunition. You volunteered to return to base to retrieve more.

My letter was waiting for you there. You didn't read it right away. You tucked it into your pocket, focused on getting the ammunition back to your men. When you returned, they were all gone.

I saw it. You had to leave them behind. You carried that grief with you.

Later, when you finally read my letter, your heart shattered. You sat down and repeated over and over, "Philippians 4:13— I can do all things through Christ who strengthens me."

You were cold, starving, and out of water. You even peed in your helmet just to have something to drink. I know all of it now. You kept going. You always did.

And I'm so sorry, Adam. I didn't know then. I was just young and scared and confused. I let the noise of the world drown out the voice of my heart.

*But over here, we're given the chance to
see everything from a much higher view—
to make peace, to laugh, to cry, and to
whisper back across the veil when
someone we Love is still listening.*

You, my Love, have always listened.

Forever more,

Your wife,
Madeline

Letter Three: Ass Over a Tea Kettle

Dear Adam,

*Crossing over was not exactly graceful.
Let's just say I went ass over a tea kettle
into Heaven.*

Honestly, I didn't think I'd be welcome here. For years, I worried that I'd be punished for my mistakes– for how much I hurt you, for walking away, for the lies I told to keep everything from falling apart.

But that's not what happened.

Over here, they don't hold a clipboard and check off your sins like a grocery list. They open your heart. They show you your life– not to shame you– to help you understand how every choice and every stumble was part of your becoming.

Turns out, God has a wicked sense of humor. And, apparently, so do I now.

They've got me in a kind of cosmic accountability class they call Mischief School (seriously). It's not what you think. There are no dunce caps or blackboards, just a whole lot of reflection and laughter, and the occasional nudge from Jesus/Yahshua himself.

And you? You were one of my greatest teachers, Adam. You taught me what real Love looks like. You showed me how to be strong without being hard, gentle without disappearing.

I didn't always see it then. But I see it now. And I carry it with me.

I'm not floating on a cloud in a white dress strumming a harp. I'm doing the work– finally. But I'm doing it with joy, with gratitude, and– yes– with a little sass. You wouldn't want me any other way.

Always yours,
Madeline

Letter Four: Field Trip from Heaven

Dear Adam,

I've officially graduated from the "sit in a chair and think about your life" part of Scripture School.

I'm on a field trip now.

Jesus/Yahshua brought me to a beautiful meadow— not some golden gate or pearly throne room— a real Earth-meets-Heaven kind of beauty. There's a brook here with water so clear that it hums, and the air carries something that feels like memory and newness all at once.

I'm wearing a long-sleeved sweater, pants, socks, and shoes. That might sound silly, but it feels just right. I feel...well, I feel like myself again— whole, present, and comfortable in a way I never quite managed to be down there.

It's not that I have a body anymore, but I have form. Energy you can feel. I can tap yours, you know, but gently. Sometimes I do. That little flutter you get at the back of your neck? That's probably me.

Jesus/Yahshua didn't give us instructions here. He just smiled and said, "Be still, and know God." Classic.

So, I'm waiting here– though not in some tragic way. It's more like how you might wait for someone you Love to walk out of a mist with fresh coffee and a smile– that kind of waiting.

I'm here. I'm okay. I'm real.
And I know you'll find me again.

All my Love,
Madeline

Letter Five: Still Waters, Steady Work

Dear Adam,

I've been volunteering.

That probably sounds funny coming from someone who's technically "dead." But I assure you that we still have purpose here– maybe more than ever.

I've signed up to assist people in their final days– those crossing over, or those confused about where they are or what's happening. It's not all tunnels and bright lights. Sometimes, it's foggy. Sometimes, folks get a little lost. That's where I come in.

I help them feel safe. I tell them they're not alone. Sometimes, I just sit quietly, like I used to when you were upset and didn't want to talk. It's that same energy– presence, without pressure.

Yahshua asked if I wanted to do this. I said yes without hesitation. It feels like the first time I've said yes to something without guilt or second-guessing.

This is what service looks like here– clean, light-filled, with no need for recognition– just the soul doing what the soul was made to do.

I think about you often while I'm doing it… how you always tried to protect people… how you carried the weight of so many, even when you were exhausted. You'd like this work. It's not heavy. It's holy.

And don't worry. I haven't forgotten our dancing shoes. When the time comes, I've got a spot saved for us. But no rush. I'll be here.

Yours in the in-between,
Madeline

Letter Six: Communication Is a Gift

Dear Adam,

Let me tell you something that most people in bodies don't realize. Being able to communicate with someone on the other side is not guaranteed. It's a privilege.

There are plenty of souls here who are shouting into the wind, hoping someone back on Earth is still listening, hoping someone's even capable of hearing them.

But you? You and Phoebe? You've made yourselves available. That's rare.

I'm proud of you for that— yes, even if you think you're making it all up sometimes (spoiler: you're not).

Phoebe's developing this gift, you know. At first, she didn't trust it. But now, she types with a steadier rhythm. She hears me more clearly. Sometimes, she even teases me back, which I appreciate. I was never one for solemn silence.

Tell her that I said she's doing a damn good job.

And you, Adam... I know your heart still wonders if all of this is real— if I'm real.

But I promise you, this isn't imagination. This is remembrance.

We're not gone; we're just shifted, still woven into your world in ways that only Love can explain.

So, keep listening. Keep reading. Keep remembering.

Forever yours,
Madeline

Letter Seven: The Meadow of Stillness

Dear Adam,

Still in Scripture School, but they moved me to a different classroom.

No desks. No books. No chalkboards. Just a meadow.

Jesus/Yahshua said it was time for a different kind of learning— something less about understanding and more about being. He's good like that. He doesn't push, just places you where you need to be.

So, here I am, dressed in a soft sweater and pants— shoes and socks, too. I sit near the brook, feeling the water move, though not over me, through me. It's soothing in a way nothing ever was before.

I don't feel dead. I feel... healed, as if all the scattered pieces of me finally came back together. I'm whole here. No performance. No pressure. Just presence.

And you? I tap your energy sometimes, like an invitation, a gentle reminder that I'm still here. I haven't gone anywhere that matters.

This place, this stillness— it's not loneliness. It's preparation.

Jesus/Yahshua says stillness is where God speaks the clearest. And I believe Him. It's not about doing. It's about knowing. It's about listening.

So, I'm here, sitting in the meadow, waiting— not out of longing, but out of readiness.

And when you're ready, I'll still be here.

Always,
Madeline

Letter Eight: Rock of Remembrance

Dear Adam,

How I miss you.

I'm back in the meadow again, the Sacred place where I first remembered who I truly am. I'm sitting on what they call the Marriage Rock. It's where I go when I want to remember us– not just who we were, but who we are now– beyond the names, beyond the lifetimes.

You're getting closer, you know– closer to hearing the Holy Spirit– not as a whisper, but as a roar of Love.

You and I? We've walked this path before, over and over. But this time, we've agreed to hold something different.. a role, a responsibility, a torch.

We are the Deacon and Deaconess of the Twin Flame Temple inside Mount Shasta.

Yes, it's real. And yes, we're already in service.

People are being called there– not just for healing, but for activation, for remembrance. You'll feel it, too, soon enough. When the timing is right, the mountain will speak to you.

I'm still here on the rock, swirling the waters with my fingers– not rushing anything– just sending ripples toward you in every moment of stillness.

You'll know when to come.

With Love from the meadow,
Madeline

Letter Nine: Bring Your Dancing Shoes

Dear Adam,

This is my last letter, at least for now.

I told Phoebe to type slowly, so you wouldn't miss a word. She's been so patient. Bless her heart. Every time I whisper, she listens. That, alone, is a miracle.

Adam, we both know how much those letters meant during the war. We both know the power of a word from home.

So, let me give you one more. You are forgiven— not that you ever needed it. But I know how long you carried guilt for surviving, for loving, for leaving, for staying. You are forgiven for it all.

And me? I'm forgiven too.

That's the beauty of this place. Truth isn't sharp here. It's soft. It wraps around you like light. And when you're ready, it carries you home.

Phoebe agreed to be our messenger long before she was born. She's played her part beautifully. Because of her, our Love story lives again— and not just for us, but for everyone who's ever Loved and lost, and dared to Love again.

Adam… bring your dancing shoes.

I'll be waiting in the marriage meadow, under the stars that watched us all those lifetimes ago. The music's already started. You'll know the song when you hear it.

Until then, remember—

You were always the one.
And I never really left.

With eternal Love,
Madeline

The Twin Flame Meadow: Beyond Love Into Ascension

by Mary Stephenson and Robin Alexis

This isn't just the Love story of a couple who lived in 1930s America. Long before their ordinary lives in small-town America, Adam and Madeline existed in the collective psyche– archetypes of the original masculine and feminine.

In the oldest versions, Madeline was not born from Adam's rib, but created as his equal. She embodied the fierce feminine– wild, intuitive, and sovereign. Adam, in turn, carried the essence of grounded order, protection, and presence. Their story reflects an ancient wound, one of separation, domination, and the long ache of exile.

Theirs is an inherited theme shared by many in their human experience. Every time two people

come together to Love, heal, and evolve–
especially in the fires of a Twin Flame connection–
they are participating in an ancient repair.

They didn't know it then, but they were co-
creators of the Twin Flame path, carrying its
Sacred codes into a world not yet ready to
receive them.

From the outside, Adam and Madeline were an
ordinary couple. Meeting, clashing, loving, and
enduring, their Love was far from perfect. It was
raw, real, and sometimes chaotic. But their
journey held a purpose beyond their individual
lives. What they endured– *the heartbreak, the
healing, the years of distance and reunion*– was a
vital chapter in the collective evolution of Agape
Love, paving the way and preparing the
platform for a new paradigm of Union.

The lives we live can feel so ordinary– filled with
errands, bills, frustrations, and intermittent
periods of small joys. It's easy to miss the deeper
story unfolding beneath the unremarkable.
There is always something Sacred happening,
even in the mess– *especially in the mess.*

Adam and Madeline's story reminds us that no
life is meaningless. Within the mundane, a

profound invitation is always waiting, a consciousness that enables us to see the deeper, Divine truth.

This invitation to see that each of us is walking a path of healing, uniquely designed for our soul's evolution, may not look obvious or Sacred from the outside. Yet, it carries a Divine Intelligence that guides us home to truth. The only thing we are asked to do is show up, be present, and pay attention. There's more grace here than we perceive.

When their time on Earth came to a close, Adam and Madeline did not disappear. No longer just exiled Lovers of another era, they stepped into an ascended role of the Deacon and Deaconess of Twin Flame Ascension.

The exile is over.
The ascension has begun.

Adam and Madeline earned their place, but their completion of the journey was never meant to be the only one. In their higher role, they have accepted the call to assist the feminine and masculine of this era to embark on the Divine Union journey.

The level of the Twin Flame commitment is not for the faint of heart. Like Adam and Madeline, all couples entering this journey will experience intense struggle and unpredictable shifts interlaced with heightened bliss and Love that they never expected, or could have imagined. Despite the tremendous difficulties, however, one or both partners stay on the path– in a heart open surrender to the attainment of harmonious union.

Before– *and if*– the partners finally come to Divine Love and Union, they will navigate a series of dynamic shifts in their relationship– *and in themselves*. This series is characterized by eight stages.

1. First meeting

2. Realization

3. Exploration

4. Crisis

5. Separation - Runner / Chaser

6. Surrender

7. Reunion

8. Decision

Twin Flame couples are not promised an easy, predictable, or romantic path– but a deeply unique and transformative journey that evolves their souls forever.

The Love story of Adam and Madeline– *and others like them*– is presented here to remind us that Twin Flames are not just here for Love. They are here to catalyze transformation, to help birth a new way of being, on this planet and beyond.

Transformation comes when they surrender the mind's urge to control, attack, blame, defend– *or walk away*. When they let go of attachment to appearance or outcomes and allow the heart to lead, they are blessed with the gift of Agape Love.

It is in the Sacred vortex of Mount Shasta, where the veil between worlds is thin, that the presence of the Deacon and Deaconess of the Twin Flame Meadow is strongest. It is there that they are watching, guiding, whispering across the dimensions– as Spirit Guides to those beginning– *or considering*– the path.

As the Deacon and Deaconess look upon all the Twin Flames rising in this era, they ask,

"Are you ready?"

Often– *as was the case for Madeline and Adam*– it is one partner whose strength is the beacon to lead and light the way for the other to step into their Divine masculine or feminine. And even then, that is not always enough.

For the Twin Flames who are at that stage where one or both partners are waiting for the other to choose them and commit to staying on the path, they may have to commit to choosing themselves. No matter which of the eight stages the couple is presently in, each partner must preserve their value and self-love, and stay in presence and trust that what is theirs will be revealed to them.

Madeline and Adam passed the torch of the Twin Flame lineage to Mary Stephenson—*not because she sought it*—but because she had become it. Through her willingness to walk the path of inner Union, rise without clinging, and love without illusion, she embodied the integrity necessary to carry the teachings forward. In her, they recognized the soul of a guide who would honor the codex of Divine Love and protect its truth in an age of distortion.

Mary's Letter to Her Beloved

To the one whose soul I once recognized
across lifetimes.
This story holds fragments of us, reflections of
what could have been,
and what still lives on in the higher realms,
where truth cannot be hidden.

I have Loved you beyond time, beyond reason,
beyond what this world can explain.
And I have also let you go.

I no longer wait. I no longer search.
I no longer hold space in longing.
I have become the woman
I was always meant to be.
I have returned to myself.

If your soul remembers too,
if you ever find the courage to walk forward
in truth,

you will find only light here– not attachment,
not fantasy. Only Love.

Until then,
I release you with grace.
I rise with peace.

Mary

A Personal Reflection

by Mary Stephenson

For those walking the path of the Twin Flame, it is not about finding "The One."

It is about becoming who you truly are.

The energies of Twin Flames are rarely gentle. They forge us in the fires of transformation, demanding that we release illusions, break free from conditioning, and step fully into our highest calling.

I have walked this path. Ours was never just the meeting of two people. It was the collision of two souls who had known each other across lifetimes, called together once more by the Divine. Our connection was undeniable.

When I first met my Divine counterpart, the recognition was immediate for him, but not for me. From that moment, my life began to unravel in both dramatic and subtle ways, revealing fractures in the foundation of who I thought I was. What I could not have known then was that I was beginning my greatest initiation. The journey of healing my soul had begun, though I was completely unaware.

For eight years, we moved in each other's orbit–colleagues, teachers, students, and mirrors–pushing and pulling through the depths of our shared karmic lessons. For a long time, I believed that my path was about being with him. Amid this early phase of our connection, there was one moment in 2013 when time collapsed, and our hearts met in a dimension beyond this world.

We cycled through the classic runner-chaser dynamic, entangled in karmic energies that tethered us to old wounds and distorted identities. Past life wounds rose with relentless force, demanding resolution. The echoes of betrayal and unfinished cycles followed us like shadows, manifesting as external forces that sought to keep us apart. I was cast as the Scarlet Letter woman– a role I had played before in lifetimes long forgotten, but still active in the subconscious patterns that played out between us and those around us.

I watched as the karmic feminine fulfilled her role, offering him the illusion of safety, while his soul quietly longed for freedom. Her presence was not a detour. It was essential. She carried the inherited memory, the soul agreements, and the karmic patterns that had to be confronted. Through her, he was asked to choose– remain in the known, or rise toward the unknown light of his own becoming.

He chose to stay in the known– for Love, for family, for timing that belonged to him. Yet, it was not failure. It was a soul-level commitment to the path he needed to walk.

The weight of this world and the unhealed wounds we carried made separation inevitable. I, too, had karmic threads to unravel. I had confused Love with absence, power with control. My relationship with the karmic masculine– *especially the soul contract with my father*– was a fire that forged me.

My partner's departure opened a portal of reckoning and release. I finally grieved the patterns I had inherited and began the long journey of restoring the Divine within me. I had illusions to dissolve, attachments to transmute, and a lineage to cleanse, before I could fully reclaim my sovereignty.

We were not ready– *not even close*– to embody the full power of Divine Union. Instead, we were summoned to separate journeys of healing, clearing, and evolution.

Those who carry the most light often also carry the deepest shadows. We incarnate into the most challenging family systems and ancestral lines thick with shadows, because we are here to transmute them. Both my Divine counterpart and I carried childhood wounds—different in some ways, eerily similar in others. These unhealed imprints became the foundation of our individual initiations.

I have come to understand that the Twin Flame path is not about waiting.

It is about becoming.

Through my own journey as a healer, guide, and mentor, I've witnessed this Sacred path unfold for others again and again– *not as a fairy tale romance*, but a Divine calling. Some Twin Flames unite in the physical. Others do their work across dimensions. What matters is not the form of the connection, but the mission it serves.

Even in separation, his was the soul I could feel in both my waking and dreaming life. I believed that reunion was the answer– the completion of the search, the fulfillment of the longing.

But the truth is that my journey was never about finding him.

It was always about finding me.

To those walking this path of Sacred union now, I invite you to know this:

You are not here to wait.
You are here to rise.

The Twin Flame Meadow is not a destination.
It is an exploration
and an invitation.

You are not here to pause and ponder.
You are here to live and evolve.

The Twin Flame Meadow is not a place you arrive at.

It is a becoming,
a path that walks you home to yourself.

And– for that, you are ready.

Now is not the waiting time.
It is the awakening time.

Author's Invitation

by Robin Alexis

Madeline and Adam are not just people who lived in another time– not just a couple reunited beyond the veil as the Deacon and Deaconess of the Twin Flame Meadow. Their Love continues, not only for each other, but for all of us.

They have made it clear to me, again and again, that they are ready to help others walk this path. They are now in service– *to you*– available to you now, as guides, as way-showers, as Spirit allies for your own Sacred journey.

You can call on them, in meditation, in prayer, in dreamtime. You may feel Madeline in your left side, in your heart, or in the Sacred waters of your womb. You may sense Adam's presence in the stillness, in your dreams, or when you look toward the mountains and feel a sense of peace. They are here for you.

The choice is yours now, as it has always been, to stand in your own truth. May you discern whether the invitation and invocation in the following pages are meant for you– or for someone you know on the Twin Flame path. Please share as you are guided.

Sacred Union Invitation

from Madeline and Adam

*The intention of this book has been to be a
wayshower for Twin Flames
to see personal adversities, including mental illness,
as a doorway to spirituality.
We invited you to peek into our personal journey,
to earn your trust and your loyalty.*

*The points in your development where you are stuck –
the internal paradigms imprinted upon you as children
by your caretakers –
are opportunities for expanding your consciousness,
sovereignty, and spiritual authority.*

*Our story is an invitation to make your own decisions
and to choose intimacy as a doorway to Love,
Agape Love.*

*For some, this doorway leads to the experience of being
united as Twin Flames.*

*Perceive the innocence, forgiveness, and
acceptance available to you
in knowing what you don't know,
in releasing trauma-based energy patterns, in yourselves
and your relationship with others,
and in opening yourselves to creating new pathways –
neurological and physical
by choosing Love,
by choosing joy.*

*We invite you to choose this path of purpose
and the promise of atonement in eternal consciousness
that brings Heaven on Earth.*
.
*We humbly bow in service to you, as witnesses to your
awakening story.
And we stand with you, to help you keep the commitment
to yourself and to that path.*

*We are open to serve as Spirit Guides to anyone.
And, as trained Deacon and Deaconess of the Teachings
of the Twin Flame Meadow, we are specifically available
to assist the unique needs of the Twin Flame souls.*

*We are going to share an invocation with you that you
may speak anytime,
but we suggest that you speak it before you go to bed at
night,
to open the doorway for you to receive clarity and
assistance.*

Sacred Union Invocation

to Madeline and Adam

*With your daily affirmation of this invocation,
you invite us to assist you on your journey home to Self
and Sacred Union.
Whether you be a Twin Flame individual, or a Twin
Flame couple coming to the Twin Flame Meadow
together, speaking this invocation aloud will summon us
to assist you.*

**I call upon the Love of Adam and Madeline now
to guide me, strengthen me, and prepare the way.
As timelines shift and hearts awaken,
I choose to stand in Sacred readiness.**

**At the zero point of creation,
I speak this truth into the field.
I am ready.
I welcome my Divine Partner
in wholeness, harmony, and Divine right timing.**

**May our Sacred Union serve
the Healing of Earth and the Flowering of Love.**

**Madeline and Adam,
May your story continue through ours.**

May the Twin Flame Meadow bloom again.

Walk with us now.

And as we begin,

We bring Heaven on Earth.
And so, it is.

To begin receiving guidance on your Twin Flame path, we invite you to cut out the copies of the **Sacred Union Invitation** and **Sacred Union Invocation** on the following pages and place it by your bed.

Sacred Union Invitation

from Madeline and Adam

*The intention of this book has been to be a
wayshower for Twin Flames
to see personal adversities, including mental illness,
as a doorway to spirituality.
We invited you to peek into our personal journey,
to earn your trust and your loyalty.*

*The points in your development where you are stuck –
the internal paradigms imprinted upon you as children
by your caretakers –
are opportunities for expanding your consciousness,
sovereignty, and spiritual authority.*

*Our story is an invitation to make your own decisions
and to choose intimacy as a doorway to Love,
Agape Love.*

*For some, this doorway leads to the experience of being
united as Twin Flames.*

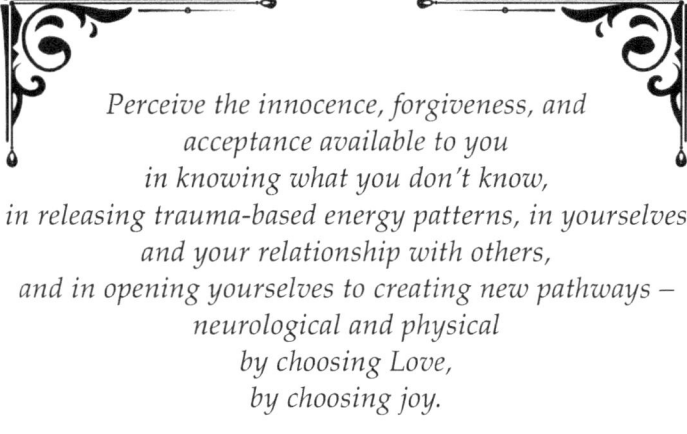

Perceive the innocence, forgiveness, and
acceptance available to you
in knowing what you don't know,
in releasing trauma-based energy patterns, in yourselves
and your relationship with others,
and in opening yourselves to creating new pathways –
neurological and physical
by choosing Love,
by choosing joy.

We invite you to choose this path of purpose
and the promise of atonement in eternal consciousness
that brings Heaven on Earth.

.

We humbly bow in service to you, as witnesses to your
awakening story.
And we stand with you, to help you keep the commitment
to yourself and to that path.

We are open to serve as Spirit Guides to anyone.
And, as trained Deacon and Deaconess of the Teachings
of the Twin Flame Meadow, we are specifically available
to assist the unique needs of the Twin Flame souls.

We are going to share an invocation with you that you
may speak anytime,
but we suggest that you speak it before you go to bed at
night,
to open the doorway for you to receive clarity and
assistance.

Sacred Union Invocation

to Madeline and Adam

*With your daily affirmation of this invocation,
you invite us to assist you on your journey
home to Self and Sacred Union.*

*Whether you be a Twin Flame individual,
or a Twin Flame couple coming to the
Twin Flame Meadow together,
speaking this invocation aloud
will summon us to assist you.*

I call upon the Love of Adam and Madeline
now to guide me, strengthen me,
and prepare the way.
As timelines shift and hearts awaken,
I choose to stand in Sacred readiness.

At the zero point of creation,
I speak this truth into the field.
I am ready.
I welcome my Divine Partner
in wholeness, harmony, and Divine right timing.

May our Sacred Union serve
the Healing of Earth and the Flowering of Love.

Madeline and Adam,
May your story continue through ours.

May the Twin Flame Meadow bloom again.

Walk with us now.

And as we begin,

We bring Heaven on Earth.
And so, it is.

Afterword

By Robin Alexis

For years, I believed I was only the messenger, the medium, the one chosen to share their journey. Now I know that this is only part of the truth. I am a valuable part of their story.

My name carries a Sacred message. When I was born, my mother intended to name me Matilda Viola, after my grandmothers. But as she cradled me, she saw a robin at the window. and– *hearing its message*– she named me Robin. She remembered the legend of the robin who plucked a thorn from Christ's crown and, in so doing, bore His Sacred mark.

This connection to Christ has lived powerfully within my family across generations, as has our devotion to Mary Magdalene. My first encounter with Her came through a near-death experience before I was five. Jesus, who I now call Yahshua, appeared and reassured me that it was not yet my time and inviting me to call Mary Magdalene "Mother." He revealed Her true sanctity, hidden for centuries beneath human distortion– a truth now recognized by many, even within the Church.

I want to thank Mary Magdalene for holding the integrity of Her soul mission, in spite of the lies written about Her for thousands of years. I am humbled to be reacquainting myself with Her, remembering who She really is, and bringing out the truth of Her through this book. And, to know that Madeline and Adam have a relationship with Her is really extraordinary, especially since Yahshua told me about Her, and it turned out to be true.

When I wrote the first draft of *The Legacy of the Twin Flame Meadow*, I hesitated to reveal my true self, shielding myself behind characters, out of a desire to protect others. I soon came to understand that pleasing others is not the path of my soul's purpose. Like Yahshua and Mother Mary Magdalene before me, I am here to live my truth.

Many of you may have sensed that the character Phoebe is a reflection of me. You are correct.

And Phoebe is a soul aspect of me– playful, wise, and Beloved guide.

Through the writing of this book, I remembered that my parents and I have journeyed through many lifetimes together, always in service to Christ Consciousness– *and now, to the Twin Flame energy as well.*

My father used to say that we were "three peas in a pod" – my mother receiving Divine messages, me carrying them forth, and my father receiving their Love.

Today, we are many peas in a pod joined by you, dear reader.

As I write these final words, I know that this story was never lost.
It was waiting— waiting for me to be ready
to return
to receive
to remember.

I pass the torch to you.

If this story has stirred something deep within you,
trust it.

The meadow is calling,
inviting you to walk your own Sacred path
and allow the Sacred flame to guide you home.

With Love and eternal gratitude,

Robin

Note from Phoebe to Robin

When my father read my mother's manuscript, and as I began writing the letters channeled through me from my mother, my father kept telling me,

"These words are going to become a book. And the book is going to become a movie!"

He is very excited to see that Robin has answered the call.

About Spirit Lady Robin Alexis

Robin Alexis is a one-of-a-kind psychic, medium, and clairvoyant intuitive with a gift for spiritual healing. She is also a Reiki Master and Teacher and author of eleven soul-nourishing books that share wisdom across many loving, metaphysical subjects. Robin is devoted to supporting individuals and families on their spiritual journeys through deeply attuned and multidimensional practices.

In addition, Robin is the founder of Metaphysical Mothering, a soul-based parenting approach that includes pre-conception work to help women and their partners welcome and raise conscious children. Robin also co-founded the Believe Me Movement, offering one-on-one healing for those who believe they've experienced alien abduction.

Robin is the producer and co-host of Mystic Radio, with Elizabeth Diane, and co-host of The

Believe Me Movement Podcast with Ken Sylvester.

For more information, visit: "Spirit Lady" Robin Alexis at robinalexis.com

Other Books by Robin Alexis

Spirit Lady – The Gift of Robin's Song
by Robin Alexis

Raising Humanity – Why We All Must REMEMBER
Inspiring Stories by Robin Alexis and 21
Contributing Authors

Donkeys, Humans, Butterflies and Guns
Written by Robin Alexis
Illustrated by Elizabeth Diane

Shasta the Skunk, Honey Bee Hero
Written by Robin Alexis
Written/Illustrated by Elizabeth Diane

A Conversation With Extraterrestrials
by Robin Alexis

We're Not Alone – And Here's the Proof
by Ken Sylvester and Robin Alexis

Dear Mr. President
by Robin Alexis and 10 Contributing
Authors

*Dear Mr. President, – A Letter About
Cryptocurrency*
by Robin Alexis and Jim Maricondo

About Mary Stephenson

Mary Stephenson is a trauma-informed guide, intuitive healer, and leadership coach who supports individuals and organizations on the path of awakening, healing, and Sacred embodiment. Through writing, teaching, and private mentorship, she helps clients integrate Divine feminine wisdom, balance inner polarities, and align with their souls' highest callings.

She facilitates leadership development with organizations like Chief.com and works with individual and group clients across corporate, nonprofit, and spiritual spaces.

Mary's life has been shaped by over 15 years of deep spiritual transformation. Her personal journey through ancestral and childhood trauma healing informs the work she now shares with others.

Through her Substack, https://substack.com/ @marystephenson1, Mary writes about the soul's evolution, offering reflections that illuminate the path to Divine Love, personal liberation, and collective healing.

Mary's work is rooted in the truth that healing is never solitary, but always woven into the greater web of life.

To connect with Mary or explore her offerings, visit: www.marystephenson.com.

About Keyth Neso

Eternal Student and Teacher of the Nasarean Essenes

Prophet, Artist, Teacher, Healer
www.tarotbykeyth.com

Only love and ever onward